First published in 2019 by Child's Play (International) Ltd
Ashworth Road, Bridgemead, Swindon SN5 7YD, UK

First published in USA in 2019 by Child's Play Inc
250 Minot Avenue, Auburn, Maine 04210

Distributed in Australia by Child's Play Australia Pty Ltd
Unit 10/20 Narabang Way, Belrose, Sydney, NSW 2085

ISBN 978-1-78628-339-9
CLP290719CPL10193399

Printed in Shenzhen, China

1 3 5 7 9 10 8 6 4 2

A catalogue record of this book
is available from the British Library

www.childs-play.com

Developed in association with Wellcome
www.wellcome.ac.uk

Initial concept by Jennifer Trent Staves and Barry J Gibbs

Wellcome exists to improve health by helping great ideas to thrive. We support
researchers, we take on big health challenges, we campaign for better science,
and we help everyone get involved with science and health research.

Up and Down Mum

illustrated by
SUMMER MACON

My mum is a great storyteller.

We have so much fun reading together.

She makes me laugh when she gets dressed up!

We both love to cook together.

Sometimes my mum gets really tired and stays in bed the whole day.

On these days I walk to school with my friends.

We went to the library last week to do some research for my science homework. Mum was so excited by all the books, she started talking very fast and loudly. Everyone kept looking at her. I wanted to hide!

The other day we went swimming.
Mum jumped into the water and got
told off. I felt very embarrassed!
And if she hurt herself, then what?

We do lots of things together.

When we go shopping I choose the fruit.
I like apples most of all!

Our neighbour Alyssa comes over to help my mum
when my friends come round. We play Princesses
and Dragons. Mum's an awesome dragon
and Alyssa's a fearless knight.
We have such fun. I love Mum!

Last night,
Mum went to stay
somewhere quiet
where she could
be looked after.

Once before, she stayed
away in a hospital. She sent
me a photo of her room,
which looked really nice.

My grandad usually comes to stay when Mum is away, but if he is busy, I can stay with friends.

I can talk to Grandad about anything. I always have lots of questions, especially about Mum. He helps me understand her, but doesn't always have the answers. We try to work things out together.

Most days are fine.
But sometimes Mum seems like someone different.
It's usually fun, but it can also be a bit scary.

"Everyone has days when they feel happier than others,
but for your mum it's more extreme," Grandad says.
"It's like she is riding on a roller coaster."

I think she is
my Up and Down Mum.

When she is happy,
it feels like she is
on top of the world
and she can do anything.

When she is sad, it feels like she is in a deep, dark hole and nothing can make her feel better.

Sometimes I feel like she's thinking too fast and can't stop.
I feel she might crash, like a runaway train with no brakes.

That is why she asks for help –
to get her moving at a safe speed.

Grandad says, "However much you love your mum and want to help, it's not your job to fix her. She needs help from people who are specially trained. They will look after her and help her manage her feelings.

Like a set of scales, it's all about balance."

I love Wednesday evenings. It's football night. I can
go even if Mum's not up to it because my friends can
take me. Sometimes she comes and watches me play.

My mum and I go to see a family therapist called Paul.
He is really kind and funny. I can talk about how I feel.
Paul helps everyone to listen to each other.

And we go for
ice cream afterwards!

My grandad showed me how to use the phone if I need help.
I have lots of numbers saved that I can call in an emergency.

There's my grandad, Alyssa, our social worker and
our best friends. When Mum is finding things difficult,
it's good knowing that I can call them and get help.

Today my mum
is coming home.
We are baking
her a special cake.

My grandad makes the best
cakes ever and Mum loves lemon!

"Doing something for your mum helps to make her happy," smiles Grandad.

"Just knowing that you are here for her helps her the most."

Mum is home and it feels just right!

Every day my mum takes her medicine. It helps her stay well.

Sometimes when I'm poorly I have medicine too,
but I never touch my mum's medicine as it's just for her.

I love having my music on loud and dancing. It's one of the things I like to do on my own. Mum can get annoyed if it's too noisy and she asks me to turn it down.

Then I try to play quietly. I still have a good time. It's just different.

Mum has her
ups and downs...

...but she is **MY** mum and I wouldn't have her any other way!

Bipolar Disorder

You may live with a parent who has bipolar disorder. These pages may answer some of your questions and help you talk about some of your feelings.

What is bipolar disorder?

Bipolar disorder is a condition that affects a person's moods. It is an imbalance of chemicals in the brain. It is unclear what causes it, but it is NOT a disease and no one can catch it. Much of the time you won't notice if someone has bipolar disorder. At other times their behaviour can be very different, and they may experience depression or mania.

Depression (low mood) can make a person feel sad, tired and worried, unable to get out of bed or go out. They may not feel like spending time with family or friends. This may last just for a few hours or go on for longer.

Mania (high mood) can make a person feel overexcited and energetic. They may not sleep or eat much, and it may feel like they take unnecessary risks. Sometimes they dress differently and say unusual things. They might talk really fast and seem distracted. However, mania can also make them feel impatient and angry. This can last just for a few hours or go on for longer.

Most of the time, people with bipolar disorder behave in the way we are used to.

How does it make you feel?

It can be confusing living with someone who has bipolar disorder as you might not be sure what to expect from day to day. You may feel angry, frightened, worried, sad or even embarrassed. It can help if you talk about how you feel.

However you feel, always remember your parent loves you.

Can my mum or dad get better?

It is not your job to look after someone who has bipolar disorder. There are lots of people who are trained to do this. Your parent can learn ways of coping with mood changes by talking with a therapist, and this may also help to give you a better understanding of what's happening. There are also medicines that make the chemicals in the brain work in a more balanced way.

What happens when a parent needs help?

Sometimes your parent might need to stay away to be cared for. This may mean someone else looking after you and so it's useful to be ready for this.

Write a plan with your parent about your school routines, what items you need to take with you and when you may be late coming home. Think about the other activities you take part in and what you enjoy doing, and make notes about these as well. All of this will help the person looking after you.

Together with your parent, make a list of phone numbers of trusted family and friends, doctors and support services and keep it where it's easy to find. If you have a mobile phone you could save the numbers there. This will help if you want to call someone for help, to ask questions and talk about how you are feeling.

It's important to take part in the things you enjoy: sports, hobbies, meeting friends and generally having lots of fun. Different activities can help develop new friendships and build your confidence, and can help you feel good about yourself.

Most of all, enjoy all the fun times you share with your parent.